Magical
Monty

Books About Monty

Magical Monty

Johanna Hurwitz

illustrated by
Anik McGrory

CANDLEWICK PRESS

For Sarah Ketchersid – she can transform an Internet
attachment into a real book. It's magical!
J. H.

For Grammy, who is magical
A. M.

Text copyright © 2012 by Johanna Hurwitz
Illustrations copyright © 2012 by Anik Scannell McGrory

First paperback edition 2013

The Library of Congress has cataloged the hardcover edition as follows:
Hurwitz, Johanna.
Magical Monty / Johanna Hurwitz ; illustrated by Anik McGrory. — 1st ed.
p.   cm.
Summary: First-grader Monty Morris gets a little more than he can
handle with his friend Joey's dogs, includes his new baby sister in
a school project, gives his mother a surprising gift, and learns that
sometimes a day filled with excitement is not the best thing.
ISBN 978-0-7636-5008-7 (hardcover)
[1. Family life—Fiction. 2. Schools—Fiction.] I. McGrory, Anik, ill. II. Title.
PZ7.H9574Mag 2012
[Fic]—dc22   2010047653

ISBN 978-0-7636-6457-2 (paperback)

13 14 15 16 17 18 BVG 10 9 8 7 6 5 4 3 2 1

Printed in Berryville, VA, U.S.A.

This book was typeset in Stempel Schneidler.
The illustrations were done in watercolor.

Candlewick Press
99 Dover Street
Somerville, Massachusetts 02144

visit us at www.candlewick.com

Contents

✿

1

Big Brother Monty

Just a few months ago, Montgomery Gerald Morris (whom everyone called Monty) was a six-year-old entering first grade.

Now the school year was moving toward its end, and Monty was getting closer to his seventh birthday. When he returned to school in the fall, Monty would be in second grade. It made him feel very grown-up. So much had happened during the past months. He had made several new friends, and he had been awarded an orange belt in karate. He had grown three inches, and he hadn't had a bad asthma attack in many, many months. The doctor said to his parents, "Maybe, just maybe, he has begun to outgrow his asthma." These were all wonderful things.

But the most remarkable thing of all was that without doing anything, Monty had gotten a sibling. He was no longer an only child. Now he was a big brother. Monty had a new baby sister named Amanda Lee Morris. And even before he'd ever seen her, Monty decided that her name was too long for a little baby. So at once he began calling her Mandy. And within hours, his parents, grandparents, aunts, uncles, cousins, and friends all referred to the new infant that way too. "Mandy. Mandy. Mandy."

Mandy had almost no hair. She couldn't speak. She could wave her hands and kick her feet, and she could cry. It wasn't very much. Monty thought it would be boring to be a baby.

It was Mandy's crying that most puzzled Monty.

"Why is she so sad?" he asked his parents. It worried him that their new baby was so unhappy. Didn't she like living with them?

"She's not sad. But crying is the only way she can express herself now. So she cries when she's hungry, and she cries when she's uncomfortable. You were just the same when you were a newborn," his father explained.

"Did I make so much noise?" asked Monty. It was hard to believe that he had ever been this little or this loud.

"You certainly did," said his mother, laughing.

Monty touched Mandy's arm with the tip of his fingers. She felt softer than the plush teddy bear that he had given her.

"Put your finger in her hand," suggested Mr. Morris the first time Monty had touched Mandy.

Monty looked at his sister's hands. They were so tiny, with a fingernail at the end of each finger. It didn't seem as if they could be real.

Still, Monty did as his father said. Instantly,
Mandy made a teeny-tiny fist and held on to
Monty's finger.

"She's squeezing me," said Monty with
delight. "I think she likes me."

"I'm sure she does," said his mother.

It was good to know that his new sister liked him. Monty was sure that he would like Mandy too. But it was disappointing that they couldn't do anything together. He had thought he would read to her. Now he saw that Mandy was too little to understand even the most simple story. He would have to wait until she got bigger. He couldn't read to her, and he couldn't play with her. She was much, much too little.

For the first week after Mandy was born, Monty's grandmother stayed to help. She cooked supper each evening and made all of Monty's favorite meals: spaghetti and meatballs, roast chicken and candied sweet potatoes. One night she made lasagna.

"You should stay all the time," Monty told her when he finished his second helping of lasagna.

"I'll be back," his grandmother promised, "but while I'm gone, you can help your mother in my place."

"But I can't cook," Monty pointed out. The only thing he could do was pour cold cereal into his bowl at breakfast time. Recently he had mastered pouring the milk into the bowl without spilling it all over the table.

"I'm sure there are other things you can do instead," said his grandmother.

At first Monty wondered what he could do. But gradually he found things that helped his mom. He brought her clean diapers and baby wipes when she needed them. He answered the telephone if he was around when she was busy nursing Mandy.

"I don't know how I would manage without you," Mrs. Morris told him.

That made Monty feel very good, and important too.

When Monty sat on the sofa, Mrs. Morris let him hold Mandy. She lay in his lap and moved her arms. She smelled of baby lotion. Monty studied her carefully. "Mandy is the only person in our family with blue eyes," he commented.

"They may not stay blue," his mother said.

"What will happen to them?" asked Monty with concern.

"Babies' eyes often change color. You used to have blue eyes when you were first born too."

Monty blinked and wondered at the mystery of blue eyes. Most of the time he didn't think about his eyes at all. It was news to him that his brown eyes had once been blue.

Just before his grandmother departed for her

home, she gave Monty a present. It was a magic set, a box filled with all sorts of things a magician might use. There was a deck of cards, a stuffed rabbit, three colored scarves, a coin and a coin box, a large, flat black square covered with cloth that opened into a top hat, a magician's wand, and a book of instructions.

"This should keep you very busy," his grandmother said. "By the time I come to visit again, you may be able to put on a show for me."

"Ohhh, that will be fun!" exclaimed Monty.

He sat down at once and began studying the book of instructions.

• • •

At school, Monty reported to his class all about the new baby. It had led to quite a discussion. Several other children had babies at their homes too, although none were as young as Mandy. The funniest thing was when their first-grade teacher, Mrs. Meaney, told the class, "I was the baby in my family."

Everyone laughed at the idea of a teacher being a baby.

But then Joey pointed out, "We all used to be babies."

That was exactly true. Yet, strangely, not one of the children could remember being a baby. They had all forgotten the time when they couldn't walk or talk or play or read or draw or write.

"I remember. I remember," called out Monty's classmate Gregory Lawson.

"What can you remember?" asked Mrs. Meaney with surprise.

"I can remember not knowing how to read."

Everyone laughed again. Gregory had been one of the last students in their class to start reading. In fact, he had begun reading only about two weeks ago. No wonder he could remember not being able to read. He still had trouble with new words, but Mrs. Meaney said the hardest part was behind him.

That afternoon, for a writing exercise, Mrs. Meaney gave the class an assignment. "Write about your favorite thing about not being a baby anymore," she told the children.

Cora Rose wrote, *I like going to school.*

Paul wrote, *It's fun to ride my scooter.*

Cindy Green wrote, *I like eating lamb chops and not mushy foods like a baby.*

Ilene Kelly wrote, *I like riding on my bike.*

Joey wrote, *I like playing with my friend Monty.*

When Monty heard what Joey had written, he took his pencil and crossed out the words on his paper. Then he wrote, *I like playing with my friend Joey.*

"But what did you write first?" Joey wanted to know when he saw the crossing out on Monty's paper but was unable to read the words.

"Never mind," said Monty. "It's not important."

"It's important to me," said Joey.

Monty thought for a moment. Then he whispered in Joey's ear. "I like being big enough to be a big brother," he said softly.

2

Monty the Magician

There had been a magic show at Monty's school on the very day that Mandy was born. Because his grandmother had him released from school early to visit his mother and the new baby at the hospital, Monty had missed the show. He had been a little bit disappointed not to see a real magician in action. Maybe that is why his grandmother gave him the magic set.

Now that he had it, Monty thought he could be a magician himself.

"It says on the box for age eight and up," Monty had noticed when his grandmother gave it to him. "I'm not even seven yet."

"That's true," she had replied. "But you're a very good reader. You're as good as an eight-year-old, if not better. I'm sure you can master all these tricks."

The box said there were seventy-five tricks for Monty to learn. That was a lot of tricks, and it would keep him very busy. Monty thought the very best thing in the box was the magician's top hat. He liked putting it on and looking at himself in the mirror. The hat made him look serious and important. Maybe next October he would wear it for Halloween.

He started reading the book that came with the set. One section was about card and coin tricks. Another section told how to make things appear and disappear. To his surprise, what Monty discovered was that there was no magic at all. Everything was just a way of fooling the audience. The coin never disappeared. It slipped from the magician's hand into a secret compartment in the coin box. Another trick had the coin slip up the magician's sleeve. If the magician held his arm carefully, the coin wouldn't fall out and it seemed to have vanished. The problem was that whenever Monty attempted the trick, the coin fell on the floor. And he never managed to open the secret compartment in the coin box either.

Monty turned his attention to card tricks. He spread out the cards on the table facedown.

"Do you want to see a trick?" he asked his mom.

"Sure," she replied.

Monty put the magician's hat on his head. Then he pointed with his wand to the cards on the table.

"Pick a card," he told his mom.

"Which one?" asked Mrs. Morris.

"Any one," said Monty.

Mrs. Morris studied the cards. Facedown they all looked identical. Mrs. Morris selected a card and showed it to Monty. It was the three of hearts.

"Now watch this," said Monty.

He picked up all the cards and stuck the three of hearts in the middle of the pack. Then he put all the cards down on the table again, facedown. "Pick a card," said Monty.

"Again?" asked his mom.

Monty nodded and grinned. "Yes. That's part of the trick."

Mrs. Morris picked out a card and showed it to Monty. It was the eight of spades.

"Now what?" she asked.

Monty didn't know what. According to his book of instructions, the card his mother picked should have been the three of hearts.

"Pick another one," said Monty. Maybe the trick would work on the second try.

Mrs. Morris selected the ace of diamonds.

The trick didn't work.

"Pick another one," said Monty. Why wasn't his trick working?

Mrs. Morris picked up the jack of spades.

Once again the trick hadn't worked.

"Pick another one," said Monty, feeling unhappy. Maybe if he were eight years old the card trick would work. Or maybe if his mom picked up enough cards, eventually she would get the three of hearts. Or she might forget which was the first card she had picked. It didn't seem like a very good trick to Monty.

Luckily Mandy began to cry in the next room. "I'm afraid I'll have to stop playing with you for now," his mother said.

Monty nodded. He took off his magician's hat and decided he should reread the instructions for the trick. Hopefully, next time it would actually work.

Rereading the instructions, Monty saw what he had done wrong. After his mother had picked a card, he should have put it in the middle of the deck but kept it sticking out just a tiny bit. When he spread the cards back over the table, he would have known which was the correct one. Then *he*—and not his mother—would select the card. Next time he did it, he would do it the right way.

A little later, Mrs. Morris came into the room holding Mandy. "Do you want to try your trick again?" she asked her son.

"Sure," said Monty. He really thought he could do it this time. He put the magician's hat back on his head.

Once again he placed all the cards on the table. "Pick a card," he instructed his mother.

Monty's mom studied the cards and picked one up. "Look," she said to Mandy. "We've got a seven of clubs." She showed the card to the baby. Then she showed it to Monty.

Monty gathered up all the other cards. He took the seven of clubs from his mother and stuck it into the deck. He left a small corner of the card sticking out. Then he began placing the cards back on the table. "I didn't use the magic wand last time," he explained to his mother. He took the wand and tapped the seven of clubs with it three times. Then he picked up the card and turned it over.

Monty was sure it was the seven of clubs. It was supposed to be the seven of clubs. Without looking at it, he turned the card toward his mom. "What do you see?" he asked her, smiling proudly at his magical skill.

"The four of diamonds," said Mrs. Morris.

"What? Let me see," said Monty, shocked. He felt like crying. He had tried so hard to get the trick right.

His mother turned the card so Monty could see it. It was the seven of clubs.

"I fooled you," said his mom.

"You did, you did. I did it! I did it! I did a magic trick!" he shouted triumphantly.

"Look what else you did," said his mom. She pointed to the baby.

Mandy was looking at Monty as if she understood what was going on. She didn't know about numbers, and she didn't know about playing cards with hearts and diamonds and clubs and spades. She certainly didn't know about magic. But she already knew her big brother, and she looked at him with a smile on her face.

"It's sort of magic when she smiles," admitted Monty.

"It's sort of magic having two such wonderful children," said Mrs. Morris, hugging her son the magician.

3

The Mother's Day Gift

The second Sunday in May was Mother's Day. At school, all the children drew and colored cards to give to their mothers.

"What about presents?" asked Cora Rose. "Shouldn't we make presents to give our mothers too?"

"I have a plan," said Mrs. Meaney. "You'll see."

This was the plan: each student was given four ice-cream sticks to paint.

"Where's the ice cream?" asked Joey.

"No ice cream today," said Mrs. Meaney.

Many of the children frowned. What good were ice-cream sticks without an ice-cream pop attached to them?

However, while the paint was drying on the sticks, Mrs. Meaney lined up her students and took a picture of each child. She had to take two pictures of Todd because he was picking his nose in the first picture.

"Your mom won't like this one," she said, showing Todd the picture before she deleted it and took a second shot.

Mrs. Meaney also had to take two pictures of Ilene Kelly because she blinked and her eyes were closed in the first picture.

"It's okay," said Ilene, shrugging. "My mom has seen me with my eyes closed thousands of times."

"So she has," agreed Mrs. Meaney. "But let's give her a picture of you with your eyes open," she said, and she took a second shot.

When all the pictures were taken and printed out, the students pasted them on pieces of cardboard, and the four ice-cream sticks surrounded the cardboard, to form a frame. So ice-cream sticks without ice cream had a purpose after all.

Monty studied his picture. It showed him smiling with his two top teeth missing. "I look a little bit like our baby," he told Mrs. Meaney. "She doesn't have any teeth either."

So now Monty and all his classmates had presents to give to their mothers on Mother's

Day. But Monty really wished that he could give his mother something more. The picture was all right. It showed him just the way he looked. But his mother could see him all the time. A present should be something different, something that she wouldn't be able to see all the time.

He discussed this with Joey.

"I want to give my mom something besides the present we made at school," he said. "Don't you want to do that too?"

"Nah," said Joey. "Your mom won't expect you to give her two presents. One is enough."

He discussed this with the twins Ilene and Arlene Kelly. Arlene had a photo in an ice-cream-stick frame, just like her sister, who was in Monty's class. It seemed each section of the first grade made the same present.

"I wonder who ate all that ice cream," said Arlene.

"Nobody, dummy," said her sister. "They sell sticks without ice cream."

"How do you know that?" asked Arlene.

"Because the sticks were all clean when we got them."

"Well, somebody could have washed them," protested Arlene. "Or maybe they just licked them clean."

"Never mind," said Monty. "I want to give my mom something besides the picture. Do you have any ideas?"

"Give her some ice cream to go with the sticks," said Ilene, laughing.

Arlene started laughing too. They both thought it was a good joke. But Monty was serious. He wanted to give his mom a real Mother's Day present.

On TV he saw ads for jewelry for Mother's Day, but he knew he would never have enough money to buy any jewelry. Then he heard an advertisement for ordering flowers by telephone. Flowers wouldn't cost as much as jewelry, he thought. His mom loved flowers. That's what he would get her!

Monty memorized the number to call. He counted out his money in his bank. He had four dollars and seventy-three cents. That should be enough, he thought. The next afternoon, while Mrs. Morris was taking care of Mandy, Monty picked up the telephone in the kitchen and dialed the number.

"Fresh Flowers for the Family," said the voice on the other end. "Sarah speaking. How may I help you?"

"Hello, Sarah," said Monty, a little shyly. "I want to buy some fresh flowers for my mom for Mother's Day."

"How lovely," said the voice. "What sort of display would you like?"

"No, I don't want a display. Just some nice flowers," Monty explained.

"Well, we have roses, or lilies, or tulips, or a combination of spring flowers."

A combination sounded good to Monty. "That's what I want," he responded. "A combination of spring flowers."

"Excellent. That's a great choice," Sarah complimented him. "Please tell me your name," she requested.

"Montgomery Gerald Morris," he replied. "But you can call me Monty, like everyone else."

"All right. And the address to which you wish these flowers to be shipped?"

Monty answered. Then the voice asked a strange question. "What sort of card do you wish to use to pay for the flowers?"

The only card that Monty had was the Mother's Day card he'd made at school. He sat silently, wondering what to answer.

"You can use American Express or MasterCard or Visa or Discover," Sarah told him. "Any of those cards is fine."

"I don't have one of those cards," said Monty.

"Mr. Morris. Can I ask you how old you are?" Sarah inquired.

"I'm six. But I'm going to be seven in August," he told her. "And I have four dollars and seventy-three cents saved in my bank. Isn't that enough? I could put it in an envelope and mail it to you right away."

There was a pause on the other end of the phone.

"Mr. Morris," the voice said. "I'm afraid that none of our bouquets are that inexpensive. Our most economical arrangement sells for just under twenty dollars, and that doesn't include the delivery fee."

"Oh," said Monty. "They didn't say that on TV. They just said you would send flowers all over the United States and that they would be cheap and guaranteed to arrive in time for Mother's Day."

"Mr. Morris. Monty," the voice said. "I'm afraid you'll have to make another plan for the holiday. But I bet your mother will be happy with whatever you give her. You sound like a remarkable young man."

Monty sniffed back some tears. They were caused by both disappointment and embarrassment. How was he supposed to guess from the television commercial how much flowers cost, and that you needed a special card to get them?

"I've got a picture that we did at school," he told Sarah. "I guess that's all I can give her."

"A picture! Did you draw it? Did you use paint or markers?" asked the voice, sounding interested.

"No," Monty explained. "It's not that kind of a picture. It's a photograph picture, and it's of me. And we made a frame out of ice-cream-pop sticks."

"Oh, Monty. That sounds lovely. I know your mom is going to be so pleased."

"Do you really think so? She loves flowers, and I thought it would be extra special if I could give her some."

"Monty, there is no flower your mom could love more than you."

"And Mandy too," Monty pointed out.

"Who's Mandy?" asked the voice.

"She's my new baby sister. She's only three weeks old."

"Well," said the voice. "Your mom is certainly a lucky woman. She has a great son like you and a new baby daughter as well. I know she's going to have a wonderful Mother's Day, and don't you worry about giving her flowers."

"Okay," said Monty. He thought a moment. "Well, good-bye, Sarah," he said.

"Good-bye, Monty," Sarah said, and there was a click on the phone.

Mrs. Morris walked into the kitchen, holding Mandy against her shoulder. "Were you just on the telephone?" she asked her son.

"Yes," Monty said. "I was talking to someone named Sarah."

"Is that a new girl in your class?" his mother asked.

"Ummm. No," said Monty. He grabbed an apple out of the fruit bowl and took a big bite. That way he couldn't talk anymore. He didn't know what he'd say if his mother asked more questions.

Luckily, Mandy was a good distraction. Monty reached up and put his finger into Mandy's hand, which was hanging over their mother's shoulder. The baby moved her head and smiled at him. Monty smiled back. Sarah was right—his mother was lucky to have such a nice new baby for Mother's Day. Still, Monty wished for something else to give his mother. If only he could wave the wand in his magic set and *abracadabra!* there would be a wonderful surprise for his mom.

On Mother's Day, Monty and all the first-graders from his school gave their mothers four painted ice-cream sticks without ice cream but holding a picture of their child. (Mrs. Kelly down the street got eight sticks and two pictures that looked exactly the same because she had identical twins!) All the mothers said they were delighted with their gifts.

An hour later, a truck pulled up in front of the Morris house with a long box addressed to Monty's mother. Mrs. Morris looked at her husband. "Oh, this is so sweet of you," she said to him as she began to open the package.

Monty's dad shook his head. "There must be a mistake," he said, rechecking the address on the box. "I didn't order anything."

The address was correct.

Inside the box was a tremendous bouquet of assorted spring flowers. There was also a small card that said, *Enjoy a wonderful Mother's Day.* The card was signed with two names: *Monty and Sarah.*

"Who's Sarah?" asked Monty's father, looking puzzled.

"She's sort of a new friend of mine," he explained. He hadn't realized what a very good and special friend she would turn out to be. Sometimes you had magic without even chanting *abracadabra,* thought Monty.

4

The Library Project

Everyone at school was talking about it. Mr. Harris, the school librarian, was putting together an exhibit of students and teachers reading.

"Have someone take a picture of you," he told the students. "Let me see where you read. It can be in bed, sitting on the sofa, lying on the floor. Wherever. I'm going to mount the pictures and line the walls of the library."

It sounded like fun, Monty thought. "When do you want the picture?" he asked the librarian.

"As soon as you can bring it in," Mr. Harris said. "But if you are going away for the weekend and you think there will be a special place where you could be photographed, then wait."

Monty wasn't going anywhere that weekend. Now that they had baby Mandy, the family didn't seem to go anywhere special. But maybe he could get his father to take his picture sitting on a swing at the playground.

He mentioned that to Joey as they were walking home from school.

"Swing? No way," said Joey. "Why don't you sit on the top of the monkey bars?"

Monty wasn't very comfortable climbing high on the monkey bars. The couple of times he had made it to the top, he had held on tightly with both hands. He certainly couldn't read or even pretend to read a book while he was on top.

When they reached their street, Joey had an

idea. "I have to walk my dogs," he said. "But after that, I'll ask my mom if I can take our camera outside. I'll take your picture and you can take mine for the library project."

"Good," said Monty. It would be fun doing his homework with Joey.

Monty stopped inside his house to drop off his backpack. His mom was holding Mandy against her shoulder and patting her on the back.

"Are you still burping her?" asked Monty. When he had left for school that morning, his mother had been doing the same thing.

"Yes," said Mrs. Morris. "Babies need to do a lot of burping."

He made a funny face at Mandy. She smiled at him and made a small burp.

"Good girl," said Monty's mom.

"I'll be going outside," Monty told her. "Joey and I are going to take pictures for a school project."

"Okay," said his mom. "Why don't you take an apple for yourself and one for Joey?"

Monty grabbed two apples and went outside. Joey waved to him.

"I'll be ready in a minute," he called to Monty. He went back into his house with the dogs, and a moment later he returned. He was holding his family's digital camera. Monty handed Joey one of the apples, and the boys sat down on the steps outside Monty's house to eat and to plan their photos.

"Sometimes I read sitting right here," Monty said.

"Boring," said Joey. "We should try and think of more interesting places."

"Like where?" asked Monty. Reading was what was interesting to him, not where he sat to read.

"Like, like, like up a tree," said Joey. He jumped up. "That's it. I'll climb up a tree, and you can take a picture of me reading up there."

Monty followed Joey across the street, toward his backyard. There was a medium-size tree with a few branches that were low enough to climb on. The boys dropped their apple cores in the trash can, and Joey handed Monty the camera. "Okay," Joey said. "I've climbed this tree lots of times. It's a cinch for me."

Monty watched as Joey climbed up. His friend was almost like a monkey going up, up, up. "Hold tight," Monty called. It would be terrible if Joey fell down while doing the school project.

"I think this is high enough," said Joey. "Take my picture."

"But you aren't reading a book," said Monty. "The picture is supposed to show you reading."

"Boy. That was dumb of me," said Joey. He began climbing down the tree. "Wait a minute. I'll go and get a book," he told Monty.

Monty waited as Joey rubbed dirt off his hands, onto his pants, and went into the house. He wondered which book Joey would bring out. As he waited, he tried to whistle. Joey had told him it was easy to do, but somehow he still hadn't mastered the skill.

A minute later, Joey reappeared. He had a large book about dinosaurs.

"I think it would be better if you were reading a book about trees," said Monty.

"I don't have a book about trees," said Joey. "Besides, I like dinosaurs more than trees."

"Okay," said Monty.

Joey climbed the tree again. He didn't go up as quickly this second time. Monty could see that it was more difficult for his friend to climb a tree when he was holding a big book.

Joey reached the spot where he was before. "Okay. Take my picture," he instructed Monty.

Monty held the camera and pointed it at Joey. "I don't know how to make it work," he said.

"You just look through that little space and push the button," Joey shouted down.

"Is it okay if I don't see anything when I look through the space?" asked Monty.

"How can you look through the space and not see anything?" Joey asked. He began climbing down the tree. "Wait a minute," he told Monty. "I'll give you a lesson. It's very easy."

Joey jumped from the bottom branch and put the book down on the ground. He took the camera from Monty. "See? You look through this part," he said. "Then you push this button here."

Monty took the camera back and looked through the space where Joey had pointed. "Okay," he said. "I think I can do it now."

Joey quickly climbed up the tree again. "All right!" he shouted. "Take my picture now."

Monty aimed the camera at Joey. Then he lowered it and called up to his friend, "You don't have the book. You left it down here on the ground."

"Oh, nuts," groaned Joey. "This is the hardest homework we ever had. It's worse than math or spelling."

Joey climbed down the tree and picked up the dinosaur book. Then he climbed up the tree again.

"Are you ready?" Monty shouted.

"Yes," Joey replied.

"Then you should open the book. You can't read it when it's closed, like you have it now."

Joey let go with one hand and opened the book. He looked down as if he was reading. Suddenly, Monty heard a crash. Joey had dropped the book, and it had landed on the ground.

"You'll have to come down and get the book again," Monty called up to Joey.

"I'm coming down," Joey said. "But I'm not going up again. I've had it. There's got to be another place to take my picture."

"You can sit on my steps," suggested Monty.

"I'll sit on your steps to rest," said Joey. "But I don't want my picture taken there."

The two boys crossed the street again and sat down on the steps. "I'm tired," Joey complained.

"We don't have to take the pictures today," said Monty. "Mr. Harris said we could bring them whenever we had them."

The boys sat together, and Monty tried whistling again. Still no luck.

The twins Ilene and Arlene walked by. "Are you taking pictures for Mr. Harris?" Ilene asked.

"Yes," said Monty.

"No," said Joey.

"We're going to have our picture taken on the weekend," said Arlene. "My father said he was going to take us to the amusement park, and we're going to sit on the Ferris wheel reading a book together. That will make a great picture."

"Yes, it will," Monty agreed. He personally didn't like Ferris wheels, but the twins were right. It would make a good picture. He could imagine it already.

Joey frowned. "A roller coaster is better than a Ferris wheel," he said.

Monty didn't like roller coasters either. "I like the merry-go-round the best," he said.

"What kind of picture are you going to take?" asked Arlene.

"It will be a surprise," said Joey.

"No fair. We told you what our picture is going to be," said Ilene.

"We can't tell you," Monty said, "because we don't—" He was going to add "because we don't know," but Joey interrupted.

"Because it's a secret. You just have to wait till the picture is up in the library."

"No fair," said Arlene as the two girls walked home.

"What are we going to do?" asked Joey. "This is such a secret that even we don't know the answer."

"I guess I'll go in and play with Mandy," said Monty. "She can't really do anything yet except eat and burp and sleep and cry. But she likes to look at me. She even smiles whenever she sees me," he added proudly. "My mom said that she'll probably learn to speak very early because I talk to her so much."

"What do you talk about?" asked Joey.

"I tell her about school and about my karate class, and sometimes I even . . . Joey. I just got a great idea for my picture. Come inside with your camera."

"What are you going to do?" asked Joey.

"You'll see," said Monty, jumping up with excitement.

Inside the house, Monty rushed to Mandy's room and got one of her baby books. Mandy was sitting in her infant seat, in the kitchen. Monty sat down next to her and opened the book. "Are you ready?" he called to Joey.

Joey aimed the camera and took a photograph of Monty reading to his baby sister.

Mandy might not know how to speak or talk or read, but her face looked very interested. It was as if she really understood the words "In the great green room . . ."

"Lucky you. You've done it," said Joey. "I still have to think of something, but I don't want to climb the tree anymore. I wish I had a baby in my house. Then I'd make you take a picture of me reading to her."

"Wait a minute," said Monty. "I can't go into your house because of your dogs and my asthma. But you could have someone in your family take a picture of you reading to Jupiter and Pluto."

"Hey, that's a great idea," said Joey.

"Wait a minute!" shouted Monty. He just had another idea. From his room he got a book to lend to Joey. The book was called *The Planets*. It would be a good joke to read about the planets to Jupiter and Pluto, even if no one looking at the picture knew about the dogs' names. And even if Pluto was no longer considered a planet.

5

Monty Marches Forth

The last Monday of May was Memorial Day. Schools were closed, and every year there was a parade down the main street of town in memory of the men and women who had served in the armed forces.

Monty always went with one or both of his parents to watch the parade. The mayor rode in a convertible car with the top down. The car was decorated with small American flags. Everyone cheered, even if they hadn't voted for him.

Then there came people carrying flags, several bands with people playing trumpets and drums and funny xylophones called glockenspiels. There were high-school girls in matching short skirts, twirling batons, men wearing kilts who played bagpipes, firemen driving old-fashioned fire trucks, Boy Scouts and Girl Scouts in their uniforms. Even the local nursery schools marched in the parade, with parents pushing their youngsters in strollers along the parade route.

"They never had little kids when I was in preschool," Monty commented last year. It didn't seem fair that when he was younger, he hadn't been included in the parade.

But then something wonderful happened. A few days before the holiday, Sensei Jack made an announcement to Monty's karate class. "This year, we've been invited to participate in the Memorial Day parade. Any students who wish to march can do so. Just show up at eight-thirty in the morning at the corner of Dubby Street and Bogdan Avenue, and be sure to wear your karate uniform. We can show the people attending the parade how many colored belts we represent."

Monty was very proud that he had achieved an orange belt. If he marched in the parade, he could show it off to everyone on the sidewalk watching the parade.

"What if it's raining?" Arlene asked the karate teacher.

"If it's raining, I'm staying home," said Ilene.

"Chicken. Do you think you'll melt?" one of the boys asked.

"I won't melt, but I won't march either," Ilene said firmly.

Monty thought it might be fun to march in the rain. Maybe they could all hold umbrellas.

"Personally, I love the rain," Sensei Jack said. "But the instructions say that if it rains, the parade will be canceled. However, the good news is that the long-range weather forecast predicts sunny skies."

The karate students burst into applause. They all agreed that it would be fun to march in the parade.

Sure enough, when Monty awoke on Memorial Day, the sun was shining. He started getting dressed in his jeans and a T-shirt when he remembered that he was supposed to wear his karate uniform. Mrs. Morris came into his room. "Leave your T-shirt on," she told her son. "You can wear it under the karate clothes. That way you'll look just like everyone else, but I won't have to worry about you being too cool."

Monty was used to his mother worrying about his health. He was too excited about the parade to waste time arguing. He put his orange belt around his waist and tied it carefully.

"Hurry, Monty," his mother called up the stairs.

And so Monty quickly slipped his feet into his sneakers and tied only a single knot. No time for double knots this morning.

Monty rushed downstairs, ready to leave the house.

"You can't go without a good breakfast," his mother insisted. "How will you have the energy to walk two miles?"

"Two miles?"

"Yes. From Dubby Street and Bogdan Avenue

to the end of the parade route is equivalent to forty blocks, or two miles."

"Wow," said Monty, impressed. Two miles seemed like a long distance. So he sat down at the table and ate most of his bowl of cereal with a banana cut up in it. He looked over at his sister.

"Will you bring Mandy to watch me?" he asked.

"We will come for the start of the parade, but I'll have to bring her home before the end," his mom said.

Finally they left the house. Monty's dad went ahead and parked their car near the end of the parade route. "That way you won't have to walk home when it's over. You'll probably be pretty tired by then."

"Oh, no," Monty insisted. "I won't be tired at all."

Monty's mom pushed Mandy in the carriage,

and just as they were starting off, Mr. Kelly pulled up in his car with Arlene and Ilene. The sisters were wearing their karate uniforms too. "How about a lift?" offered Mr. Kelly.

"Good idea," agreed Monty's mom. "Save your energy for the marching," she told her son. "I'll wave to you when you pass by."

So Monty and the twins drove off, and Mrs. Morris walked on, pushing Mandy in her carriage.

The parade began at 9:15 a.m. There were loads and loads of people waiting to begin the march. The karate students stood together.

"White belts first," called out the sensei. Those were the beginners who hadn't been studying very long. Monty remembered back when he had been a white belt.

"Yellow belts next," called out the sensei. This was the next group of students. Monty remembered back when he had been a yellow belt.

"Orange belts next," called out the sensei. Monty stood tall and proud. The mayor's car started off, followed by the flag carriers. The first band began marching and playing their instruments.

"Remember, it's left-right, left-right. Keep in step. And keep your heads high," called out a woman who was one of the organizers. She was carrying a clipboard and checking off the groups.

"All right. Off you go!" the organizer shouted to the karate students.

All traffic had been halted. There were no cars on the street, only marchers. Monty felt very proud. He had never imagined he would be in a parade. It sure made him feel important. He kept his head high, as he had been instructed, and whispered to himself, "Left-right. Left-right." He could hear the marching tunes that the bands were playing, and it made him want to march and march forever. Marching was so much fun, and it was so easy, he thought.

Monty turned his head a little to see if he could find his mother among the people watching the parade.

"Hi, Monty!" called a voice.

Even without seeing her, Monty knew it was his mom who had shouted.

He wanted to wave, but he didn't. However, he did permit a large grin to cross his face.

Sensei Jack was marching alongside his students. "Attention!" he shouted. "Five jumping jacks."

At once all the students raised their arms and demonstrated their jumping jacks.

"Are you getting tired?" a voice asked Monty.

It was Ilene. "Oh, no," he told her. "What about you?"

"I'm tired," she said. "I wish the parade was over."

"Not me," said Arlene.

"I bet you are tired," said Ilene. "You just won't tell."

"Am not. I could walk a hundred miles."

"A hundred miles. We'd be dead by then."

"No talking," Sensei Jack called out. "Eyes front. Just keep walking."

Monty was glad that he was wearing his sneakers. When the students had karate class, they were barefoot. It would be hard to march two miles without any shoes.

But in the next moment, Monty was sorry he was wearing his sneakers.

Someone marching behind him accidentally stepped on the heel of Monty's sneaker, and suddenly his right foot was half in and half out of his footwear.

"Sorry, I gave you a flat tire" said the person behind him.

A flat tire was what the kids called making someone's shoe come off.

Monty tried to get his right foot back into the sneaker as he marched along, limping, with his foot half out of his sneaker. He couldn't. Maybe he would march better if he took the sneaker off and put it back on properly. Planning to pick it up, he managed to kick at his right sneaker with the left one, and he succeeded in getting his foot out of the sneaker. But before he could even bend down to get it, someone else kicked the sneaker farther

down the street. Now Monty was marching with one sneaker on and one sneaker off.

He hoped someone would pick it up and pass it back to him. However, instead, it seemed that whoever saw the sneaker gave it a kick. The sneaker was making its way along the parade route, and Monty was marching with a sneaker on his left foot and nothing but a sock on his right.

Marching in the parade was no longer so much fun after all. The foot without the sneaker felt every bump and pebble on the street, and that didn't feel good. Would this parade never end?

No one seemed aware that Monty had only one sneaker until he suddenly heard a loud whistle and then a voice calling out, "What happened to your sneaker?"

It was Joey. Maybe no one else had noticed, but Monty's friend had.

It was bad enough that he had to march this way. Now everyone looked at the feet of the marchers to identify him. So he tried calling out an explanation. But Sensei Jack suddenly became aware of his student.

"Don't worry, Monty. Only a few more blocks!" he shouted.

How wonderful, Monty thought. The parade was almost over.

"I'll never walk again," said Arlene.

"See. I knew that you were tired," said Ilene.

"We're all tired," said Sensei Jack. "Come on. We're almost there.

And finally, there they were, at the town green, where the parade concluded. There were two women giving out cardboard containers of orange juice. "Thanks for participating," they told the children.

One of the women was holding a sneaker. "Did anyone lose this?" she asked.

Monty came forward.

"You won't have to try this on like Cinderella," the woman said. "I can see that it's yours."

Monty blushed as he sat down on the curb and put his sneaker back on his foot. This time he tied it with a double knot. Then he opened his container and pushed the little straw inside. The cool juice felt wonderful going down his throat. It was orange, just like his belt, but he knew he would have enjoyed it no matter what flavor or color it had been.

"Here I am, Monty. Ready to go home?" called out Mr. Morris.

Monty ran over to his dad. "I lost my sneaker, but I still marched the two whole miles," he reported.

Mr. Morris looked down at his son's feet. "Well, I see that you found it again," he said. Then he called to Ilene and Arlene because he had offered to take them home for their father.

The three children threw away their empty juice containers and collapsed onto the backseat of the car.

"I'm never doing that marching again," said Ilene.

Monty was just about to agree with her, but his father spoke first.

"Oh, I bet you will," said Mr. Morris. "After all, it will be easier next year."

"Why?" asked Monty.

"Next year you'll be so much bigger. Next year you'll be in second grade."

"Wow. Second grade," said Arlene.

"Okay," said Ilene. "I guess it won't be so hard when I'm in second grade. I'll march next year too," she agreed.

"Me too," said Monty. *Next year I'll tie my laces better and make a double knot,* he thought. *Then my sneaker won't come off.* He wondered what color karate belt he would have by May of next year.

6

A Quiet Day

It was a Saturday in June. Mandy was already two months old, and for Monty it was just two months before his seventh birthday. There were only two more weeks of school until he finished first grade. He hoped he would like second grade as much as first.

Monty was sitting on one of the steps in front of his house. He had the book of instructions from his magic set in his lap. Monty still hadn't mastered the trick of making a coin disappear.

Today wouldn't be a good day to practice sliding a coin up his sleeve because he was wearing a short-sleeved T-shirt. Maybe, however, he could figure out how to use the coin box.

Monty removed the blue plastic box from his pocket. He slid it open and inside there was a fake penny also made of plastic. The instructions said to remove the coin and show it to his audience. That part was easy. But how could he put the coin back in the box and make it disappear?

It seemed to Monty that he had already read the instructions a hundred times. He sighed. Maybe reading the instructions for the one hundred and first time, he would learn what to do. He read slowly. *Put the box behind your back while you are speaking to your audience. Slid the secret panel open and place the coin inside. Close the box. Turn around. Then show it to your audience.*

His mother was sitting beside him pushing the carriage with Mandy inside. She pushed it back and forth waiting for the baby to fall asleep.

"Babies sure sleep a lot," said Monty, looking up from the secret coin box.

"Not at night," said Mrs. Morris with a sigh.

Monty had been amazed to learn that every night while he was sound asleep, Mandy woke crying, demanding to be fed.

"How come I never hear her?" Monty had asked his parents.

"Because you're sound asleep. And hopefully before long Mandy will sleep all night long too. Babies do a lot of their growing when they sleep. And besides, they are too little to do any of the things that you can do when they're awake."

Monty grinned at the thought of Mandy trying to ride a scooter. She still couldn't walk. She couldn't even sit up yet. He stood up and peeked into the carriage. Mandy saw him and waved her arms.

"Don't distract her, please," said Mrs. Morris. "I want her to get a good rest."

Monty sat down on the step again. He looked across the street at Joey's house but he knew that

Joey wasn't home. He'd gone with his family to visit relatives in another town. Monty knew that the twins weren't home either. They'd told him where they were going but he couldn't remember.

Monty sighed. He wished his sister were big enough to play with him. It seemed to him that by the time she could play games, he'd be in high school. "I wish something exciting would happen," he said, looking up and down the street. It was very quiet. An occasional car drove past but there were no people walking. Everyone was either inside their house or out for the day.

"The best days are when nothing exciting happens," Monty's mom said. "It was exciting when you were rushed to the hospital a couple of years ago with a bad asthma attack. But it's much better when you get through the day without sirens and ambulances and emergency rooms and things like that."

Monty nodded. "I don't want *that* kind of excitement. I'd like a good excitement."

"It was exciting when Mandy was born," said Mrs. Morris. "But we couldn't manage a new baby every day."

Monty giggled. It would be funny if their house were filled with new babies.

"Can I push the carriage?" he asked his mother.

"Sure," she said.

Monty put the blue plastic coin box into his pocket. Then he reached for the handle of the carriage and pushed it back and forth the way his mother had been doing.

"Do you think Mandy can tell the difference when I push her and when you push her?" he asked.

Mrs. Morris shrugged. "Probably not," she said. "I think she's half asleep already."

Monty pushed some more.

Mrs. Morris kicked at the brake with her foot. The carriage stopped moving. "All right," she said. "Mandy is asleep. She'll probably sleep for the next hour or even hour and a half."

Monty sighed. He looked down at the book of magic instructions. His scooter was inside the house, so he could always take a ride. Still, he still felt it was going to be a long and boring afternoon.

"When will dad be home?" he asked.

Even though it was Saturday, when he usually stayed home, Mr. Morris had needed to go into his office that day.

"Maybe in another hour," said Monty's mom. "I bet he'll take you to the playground when he gets home," she told her son.

Monty nodded. Sometimes an hour went by very fast, like when he was playing with Joey.

And sometimes an hour seemed to take forever, like right now.

"I think I'll get my knitting," said Mrs. Morris. "Will you watch Mandy while I run into the house?"

"Sure," said Monty.

Mrs. Morris got up from the step and went into the house. Monty stood and peeked in the carriage. Mandy was fast asleep. He tried to push the carriage a little, but because the brake was on, it didn't move. He kicked at the brake and released it. Then he could move the carriage back and forth just a little. It would be fun to walk down the street pushing the carriage, he thought. Mandy wouldn't even know, and he didn't think his mother would mind. She often walked up and down the street pushing the carriage.

Monty started off. Suddenly he felt a tickle in his nose. Instinctively he lifted his hands to cover his nose and keep the germs in his sneeze from going toward the baby. But when he removed his hands from the handlebar, the carriage began moving down the street on its own. It went at a more rapid pace than when Monty had been pushing it. Monty sneezed and ran at the same time. He had to catch up with the carriage.

Somehow despite all the thousands of times he had walked or ridden his scooter down the street, he had never noticed the slight incline. The carriage rolled faster and faster. Monty raced after it.

"Oh no," Monty cried aloud. His sister was asleep inside the carriage. He had to catch it and rescue her before there was a crash.

"Monty!" a voice shrieked loudly. It was his mother.

She was running down the street toward Monty, who was running down the street toward the carriage.

"Mandy!" shrieked another voice.

It was Monty's father, who had just pulled

up in his car beside their house. He jumped
out and ran down the street toward Mrs. Morris,
who was running down the street toward Monty,
who was running down the street toward the
carriage.

But just then, Monty noticed something. The carriage was slowing down because the incline in the sidewalk had ended. He caught up with the runaway carriage and grabbed the handle. He peeked inside. Mandy was still fast asleep. She didn't even know what an adventure she'd just had.

Mrs. Morris caught up with Monty and the carriage, and a second later Monty's dad caught up with all of them.

"It's all right," said Monty, gasping for breath. "Mandy's okay."

"Are you all right?" asked his mother as she caught her breath.

"Yes, yes," Monty assured her.

Mrs. Morris turned the carriage around, and she and Monty's father and Monty, along with Mandy in the carriage, slowly walked back to their house.

"Oh, look!" screamed Monty, pointing to their car.

The car was slowly moving down the street, although no one was inside driving it!

"Oh, my heavens!" shouted Mr. Morris, running after his car. Luckily he caught up with it, and luckily no one had gotten hurt by the runaway car. "I was so worried about the carriage rolling down the street and both of you chasing after it that I just jumped out of the car," he explained when he returned to them. "I don't know which is worse: a runaway carriage or a runaway car."

"It's all right," said Mrs. Morris. "They both were stopped, and no one got hurt."

She pushed the carriage to the front of their house and put down the brake. "Now I'm going to do my knitting," she announced as she sat down on the step.

"I'll go fix myself a sandwich," said Monty's father. "And then I'll take you to the playground if you'd like."

"Sure," said Monty, sitting down next to his mother.

"You know what?" he asked her.

"No. What?" she inquired.

"We had an exciting afternoon after all."

"Yes, we did," said Mrs. Morris. "And wasn't I right? It's much better not to have exciting times."

"It's okay," said Monty. "Mandy is still sleeping. She wasn't scared at all when the carriage rolled away."

"Well I was," said Monty's mom.

"So was I," admitted Monty. "And I was scared when our car rolled away too."

"Me too," said Mrs. Morris. She put down her knitting and hugged Monty. "All's well that ends well," she told him.

Monty nodded. He took the little box from his pocket and looked at it once more. He turned the box around. Then he slid his fingers from side to side. And suddenly, for the first time, he was able to slide the box open. Boy was he dumb! He'd been holding the box the wrong way. It wouldn't work unless he held it upside down. The instructions had told him to turn it around but he thought it meant *he* should turn around.

"I did it!" he exclaimed with delight. He wondered if he could do it again. It would be terrible if he couldn't. He took the coin from the box and held it up in the air. "Mom, watch me. I think I can do the coin trick." Then he put the box and the coin behind his back and slid the box shut. "Now watch," he said.

He opened the box and there was no coin inside. "I did it!" he exclaimed.

"Can you find the coin again?" asked his mother.

Monty closed the opening. Then he put the box behind his back and turned the box around so it would be upside down. "Abracadabra," he said. He showed his mother the box, and as she watched, he slid the secret opening. There was the coin!

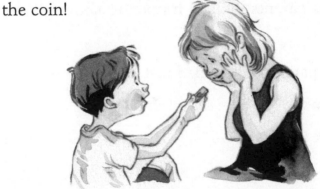

Now that he knew how to do it, it was very easy.

Mr. Morris came outside. "Dad!" shouted Monty, forgetting to keep his voice down. "I can do it!" he shouted in triumph. "I can make the coin appear and disappear. Watch!"

He repeated the trick again for both of his parents. First he opened one side and put the coin into the box. He closed it and put the box behind his back. Then he turned the box upside down and opened the box. It was empty.

"Now watch," said Monty. He put the box behind his back again. And when he next showed it to his parents, he slid it open to show off the coin.

His parents applauded just as if they were at a real show.

"Good for you," said Monty's father. He took the coin from Monty. "Do you want to buy an ice-cream cone with this?" he asked.

"Dad, you know that isn't real money," said Monty.

"You're right," said his father. He jiggled some coins in his pocket. "I don't have magic money, but I think I know how to do a magic trick. I can transform the money in my pocket into two ice-cream cones on the way home from the playground."

"Yippee!" shouted Monty. "Oh, did I wake Mandy?" he asked his mother.

"No. She's still asleep," said Mrs. Morris, smiling at him.

"Dad, can we bring an ice-cream cone home for Mom?" Monty asked his father.

"Sure."

"That will be a great trick," said Monty. He could already imagine the taste of the ice cream in his mouth. Imagination was a kind of magic too. Everyday life was full of all kinds of magic, he thought.

Monty's friends Arlene and Ilene have their own adventures in:

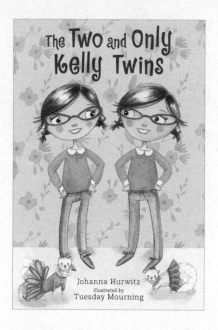

Second-graders Arlene and Ilene Kelly are identical twins and they love being a pair: they dress alike, they have identical pet ferrets, and they do everything together. But being a twin is not always easy.

Available in hardcover and as an e-book

www.candlewick.com